THE SECRET EXPLORERS

AND THE CAVE CRISIS
THE

T0368747

CONTENTS

Chapter One
GLOW IN THE DARK

Leah looked up at the evening sky, hoping it would soon be filled with bats.

She chuckled. That made her sound like a witch! But although some people did think bats belonged in spooky stories, Leah thought they were wonderful.

She'd read all about them, and was keen to see these little flying mammals with her

own eyes. So, to encourage a colony to visit her garden, she had hung bat boxes on the trees. It could take months for bats to move in, and so far she hadn't seen or heard a peep. But she had a feeling that tonight was the night. The sky was clear, the air was warm, and there were bugs everywhere – a bat's favourite snack.

"Come on, you little bat-lings!" she whispered. "It's dinner time!"

As the sky melted from blue to black, she listened for the flap of papery bat wings, watching for the dark shapes that blinked in and out of the shadows. Then something caught her eye. A flash of green. Was it light reflecting off a bat's eye, perhaps? No, there it was again! More of a glow than a flash, and it was coming from the bottom of the garden. Leah went to investigate.

Whatever was creating that light appeared to be attached to the garden shed door! Being a biology expert, she knew there weren't many animals that created the bright glow known as luminescence, and bats definitely couldn't glow. Perhaps it was a glow worm? She didn't want to disturb it if it was trying to attract tiny insects for a meal, but what sort of biologist could resist seeing something so remarkable close-up?!

She tiptoed closer and closer...

"Oh!" she cried with delight. The light wasn't coming from an animal. It was a small glowing disc, marked with compass points. It was the very same symbol as the badge she wore on her top – the mark of the Secret Explorers.

The Secret Explorers were a group of eight curious children who teamed up to solve mysteries, and the glowing disc was a portal, and a sign that there was work to do.

"I've been lured to an Explorer mission like an insect to a glow bug!" she laughed.

Leah looked back up the garden, hesitating to leave her bat-spotting session. But then she remembered – time stood still when she was away. If the bats were there, then they'd still be there when she returned.

"Back soon, my *chiropteras*," she said, using the scientific name. *Chiroptera* meant 'hand-wing', and it referred to the webs of skin that connected the fingers and thumbs of the bats' hands. "But now, I've got to fly!"

Leah opened the shed door and was blinded by a flash of white light. On the other side, she emerged into a cool room. Even before her eyes adjusted, she knew where she was. The Exploration Station had stone walls lined with computers, and glass cabinets displaying mementos from the Secret Explorers' travels: ammonites and seed pods, moon-rock and machine parts, dinosaur bones, and ancient scrolls. On the ceiling was a map of the Milky Way; and on the floor, a giant map of the world. Who knew where on that map the next mission would be? It was time to find out.

"Here!" called Leah, kicking off the roll call.

"Here!" said Gustavo, the history Explorer, who appeared through the portal in a Tudor ruff. "Stylish, don't you think?"

"Here!" said Ollie, squelching through the door in damp shoes. He was the rainforest Explorer.

"Here!" said Kiki, the engineering expert, trailing a measuring tape.

"I'm here," said Tamiko, the dinosaur Explorer, wearing a fossil-patterned t-shirt.

"Hi," said Connor. The oceans expert was picking seaweed out of his pockets.

"Here," said Roshni, the space Explorer. "Am I light years too late?"

"No, you're just on time," Leah laughed. "Who are we waiting for?"

The Secret Explorers looked at each other and yelled, "Cheng!"

"Here!" The geology Explorer entered wearing headphones.

"Are you listening to rock music?" Leah asked. Everyone laughed.

"It was a podcast about soil erosion, actually." Cheng winked.

"Well, now that we're all here, what's our mission?" Leah said eagerly.

"And where!" said Kiki.

They looked up at the Milky Way and then down at the world, where a little light was flashing on the map.

"That's India!" Roshni exclaimed. "That's my country!"

A screen popped up from the map, showing a dark cave. Inside it was a flashing light. A cave and a blinking light. *Aha! Perhaps, this time it really is a glowworm!* Leah thought. But as the picture became clearer, the Secret Explorers could see that there was a young woman in the cave, and the light was shining from her torch.

That's the second time today I've been tricked by a glowing light! Leah chuckled to herself. Clearly this mission wasn't about luminescent bugs! She looked closer at the image.

"I think the woman in the cave is signalling for help," Leah said.

"That must be our mission – to rescue her," said Ollie.

"Who knows about caves?" said Tamiko. "I mean, I know a little bit."

"Any one of us," Gustavo said. "Caves have played an important part in history, from cavemen to pirate smugglers."

"And there are caves made by people, which require precision engineering," Kiki said.

"And there are underwater caves," Connor added. "And forest caves," he added, looking back at Ollie.

And caves have incredible ecosystems, Leah thought to herself. As if the Exploration Station could read her mind, her compass badge lit up. It meant that she was going on the mission.

"It's me!" she declared.

The Explorers cheered and then waited to see who would be chosen to go with her. A mission always required two people out in the field, while the others stayed at headquarters, ready to provide backup.

Cheng's badge lit up. "Looks like it's biology and geology!" he said with glee.

"Let's get this show on the road! That is, if the Beagle is going by road!" Kiki said, pulling a lever.

The floor parted, and through it rose an old go-kart. But the Beagle – named after the ship of the famous naturalist Charles Darwin – was not only reliable, it was worldly. It could take the Explorers as high up and as deep down as they needed to go.

Leah and Cheng jumped into the seats as their friends took their places at the computers.

"Ready?" said Leah.

"Steady," replied Cheng.

Together they pressed the start button and said, "GO!"

Travelling by the shape-shifting go-kart could be uncomfortable, so Leah gripped her seat tightly, preparing for the shake and rattle. But there was no shuddering and clanking, and no transforming. There was just a blinding bright light. When they opened their eyes, the Beagle was parked on stony, uneven ground. Below them was a wide view of the treetops and fields below. They could see they were in a hilly region, but that's all they knew.

"Where are we?" Cheng said, looking out across a rocky landscape.

"Turn around, Cheng," Leah advised. Just beyond them was the mouth of a very large cave.

Chapter Two
READY, STEADY, CAVE!

"Brilliant! We're already in the right gear for caving," Cheng said, feeling the helmet on his head.

Leah checked her clothes. Just like Cheng, she was wearing sturdy boots and waterproof clothes with knee and elbow pads. At their feet were backpacks.

"Is this all we need?" she said a little nervously. "I've never explored a cave before."

"Don't worry, I've done it plenty of times," Cheng said with an encouraging smile. "Let's just make sure our bags have all the essentials. Being unprepared is the biggest danger of all."

Cheng and Leah untied their backpacks and rummaged inside.

"Ropes, harness, first aid kit, whistle... and what's this?" Leah asked, holding up a handful of plastic pointy hooks.

"Those are markers," Cheng said. "You lay them along your route, pointing in the direction of the exit so you can find your way out.

Caving can be extremely confusing – it's easy to lose track of which way you go, especially when there are lots of tunnels to choose from."

Leah felt a shiver run down her spine. Imagine being deep in a cave without any way of knowing which way to go!

"Okay, all set," said Cheng.

"Wait a minute. I can hear voices."

A group of people was approaching, all dressed in similar clothes to them, and listening carefully to a man at the front. From his reassuring voice, Leah and Cheng guessed that he must be a tour guide. "Now, we're just arriving at the mouth of the Blue Caves. So long as you follow the instructions, you'll be absolutely fine," said the man. "If you have any questions, I'm here to help."

"Let's talk to him," Leah said. "He might be able to give us some advice about the caves."

"Any extra information would be good before we enter," said Cheng.

The tour guide was small and wiry, with lively eyes. "Are you supposed to be with my group?" he asked. "If so, you were meant to sign in and meet us at the caving centre."

"No, we're not tourists. We're here to find a woman who's trapped in the caves," explained Cheng.

The man stepped back, alarmed. "Are you sure?" He shook his head and sighed. "We are low on staff at the centre. I wonder if a name got missed off the register?" He checked his clipboard and counted the people in his group. "No, it looks as if everyone is here."

"Can we go in and check, just in case?" Cheng asked.

The guide's eyes widened. "No, no, no. Unless you are with a professional guide, it is far too dangerous to enter the Blue Caves. This cave system is vast. Most of it hasn't even been mapped yet."

"Perhaps you could give us some information," Cheng said hopefully.

The man laughed. "It would take a week just to tell you what I know about the first few chambers, and even then, you wouldn't be prepared for the possible hazards inside."

"Then, why don't we join your group?" Leah said brightly.

"I think that's a very good idea. My name is Hunar," the man said, nodding. He held out his hand.

"I'm Leah," Leah said, shaking it. She noticed the roughness of his fingers from years of caving. "And this is Cheng."

"Pleased to meet you, Leah and Cheng. Now, I'd better get this group organized for their tour. You're welcome to join us."

As Hunar turned to check his group's equipment, the Secret Explorers looked at each other with raised eyebrows.

"Hunar is a professional," whispered Leah. "I can't imagine him losing anyone. Do you think there really is a missing person?"

"The Exploration Station never gets it wrong," Cheng said with a shrug.

Leah nodded. "Then maybe she went in alone. And if Hunar hasn't come across her, maybe she's gone a different route."

"And some of the cave system is still unmapped..." Cheng said. He shook his head with worry.

As they were talking, Hunar's party entered the cave mouth in front of them, and Leah and Cheng followed.

"Now, everyone, listen carefully." They were barely inside the first chamber and Hunar's voice echoed like they were in a cathedral. "These aren't just empty tunnels. They are a home to living creatures. There's an entire ecosystem that inhabits the caves."

Leah's heart was thumping with anticipation, but hearing Hunar speak about the biology inside the caves gave her a burst of excitement.

"Can anyone tell me what creatures live here?" Hunar asked.

Leah wanted to give someone else a chance, but when no one spoke, she decided to share her knowledge. "There are usually bats in caves, and their guano – that's poo – provides nutrients for the insects."

"Absolutely right," Hunar said. "And this entire ecosystem is delicately balanced, which is why we must tread carefully. We are concerned that the bat population has somehow been disturbed. There aren't as many now as there used to be."

"Why, are there predators?" Leah asked.

"One theory is that the caves have become infected with a fungus from outside that is bad for the bats – that's why we ask you to check your shoes for mud and dirt before we go further, especially if you've recently been in other caves that may be infected." Hunar clapped his hands to show it was an instruction.

"You're clean," Leah said, checking Cheng's soles. "But I think we now know why the Exploration Station chose me."

Cheng nodded. "Endangered bats, sharp rocks, and a lost woman," he mused. "This mission is going to need all our biology and geology skills. Perhaps we should warn the Secret Explorers so they can get up some information on the computers. I'll tap it into the console on the Beagle."

"Great idea," Leah agreed.

Cheng stuck his head out of the cave mouth and quickly returned. "The Beagle's gone!"

"It'll turn up when it's ready," Leah said. "It always does. Come on, the others are moving."

The group followed Hunar through the first cave and then down darker passages, where only small amounts of natural light broke through holes in the ceiling. The narrow paths opened up into a series of larger rooms, some with high ceilings and others with ascending ledges that jutted out into the space-like balconies.

"With all those balconies, they look like theatres," Leah said, mouth gaping.

"Rock formation is really interesting," Cheng said, running his hand along a section of wall. "Touch this... Can you feel how smooth it is? It's probably worn down over centuries by trickles of water, or maybe by bacteria eating away the soft stone."

"Bacteria?" Leah said brightly. Bacteria was definitely a biologist's business.

"Maybe," Cheng said. "I don't know enough about these caves to be sure, but I'd love to find out what kind of rock this is and whether it's full of minerals. I wonder if we'll see stalactites."

Leah looked up. She didn't spot any of those strange rocky spikes on the cave ceiling, but she did see something else hanging down. Dark oval shapes, dangling like the exotic seed pods Ollie had brought back from Australia. Leah tried not to squeak with excitement. They were bats! But what sort?

Someone ahead of them tripped and let out a shriek, and the noise made the bats rustle irritably. One's head emerged from the cover of the tight cloak it had created with its wings, and Leah could clearly see the big pointy ears and stubby nose.

"Look, Cheng. Horseshoe bats!" Leah said, pointing wildly.

"Wow!" Cheng nodded. "You even know the species. That's cool!"

"So I *did* get to see bats today!"

"What?"

"Never mind," Leah laughed. "I just had a mission of my own before I got called into this one."

The further they moved into the caves, the darker it became. They turned their head torches on. The flicker of the light on the walls was eerie, and Leah noticed that members of the group started walking closer together. She couldn't blame them. The idea of getting left behind was scary.

They passed the entrance to another cave on their right, which was roped off. Someone in the group spoke. "Why can't we go in there? Is it to protect us from something dangerous?"

"It's protecting the ecosystem from something dangerous – us!" Hunar said. "Come. This way."

The crowd shuffled past, but something inside the forbidden cave caught Leah's eye. It was a bright piece of plastic. A marker. Someone had been that way!

Chapter Three
THE FORBIDDEN CHAMBER

Leah looked at Cheng – he had seen it too.

"Someone was marking the way," he whispered. "But why would they go in there, if it's roped off?"

Above them came a beeping sound.

"Beeping bats?" Cheng said.

Leah swallowed her laughter before it burst out. "Bats do squeak for sonar location. They send out a noise and measure how long

it takes for the noise to bounce back. But that," she giggled, "is too beepy for a bat!"

"Well whatever the beep is, it's hanging out with the bats," Cheng said.

Leah peered up, and her helmet light flashed off a metal body and glinted as it hit the whirring blades of two tiny propellors. "Wait, I see it. It's some kind of drone," she said.

"And I bet you that's a drone called the Beagle!" laughed Cheng.

As if it could hear its name, the drone beeped again, then blinked red and blue.

"It's keeping an eye on us," Leah said. "Come on, let's find out more about this strange marker."

"But we can't let the others see us. They might follow."

Most of the group was listening to Hunar's explanation of the cave structure, but some were looking back towards the roped-off cavern, still curious about the forbidden chamber beyond.

The Beagle beeped again – loudly.

"What was that noise?" said a young

member of the group.

"Was it a bat?" said another.

The tourists looked up and spotted the colony above their heads.

"Look at all the bats!" someone called. "They're beeping!"

"Hunar, can bats beep? Are beeping bats native to this area?" said an older man with a long white beard.

Hunar blinked with confusion. "I – I – I don't think... Let's take a look."

The group rushed to stand beneath the mysterious beeping bats, and Leah and Cheng looked at each other and grinned.

"Beep beep!" Cheng said.

"Come on. Quickly."

While everyone's attention was caught by the Beagle's clever distraction, the Secret Explorers ducked under the rope and entered the cave beyond.

Away from the group and their cluster of head torches, they found themselves in dank, musty gloom – the thin beams of the Explorers' head lamps were the only light to see by – and Leah's skin suddenly shuddered with goosebumps. She pushed her fear aside and focussed on the mission.

They crouched to look at the green marker. There was another further along. And another.

"There's a trail of them. Someone knew what they were doing," Cheng said.

"Let's follow them. Head torches on full beam!" Leah said.

Scanning the walls and ceilings they edged deeper and deeper into the cave system, thankful of their warm jackets as the temperature dropped.

"Underground, the temperature remains quite constant," Cheng said. "It won't get colder than this."

"Good, although I hope the lost woman has something warm to wear."

As they made their way through the chamber, Leah noticed the thick layer of bat droppings on the walls and ground.

"Cheng, look at this. It's all dried up," she said, kicking at the crusty black pellets.

"Good. I don't fancy walking through the fresh stuff," Cheng said.

"It's not a good sign. It means that there haven't been many bats down here in a long while. And if there are fewer bats, and less poo, then there's fewer nutrients for the other creatures that live here."

"Who would have thought poo was so important!" Cheng laughed.

"Guano – that's poo from seabirds and bats – is an amazing food and fertilizer," Leah said. "Did you know guano was so important to the Inca Empire in South America for their crops that they passed laws

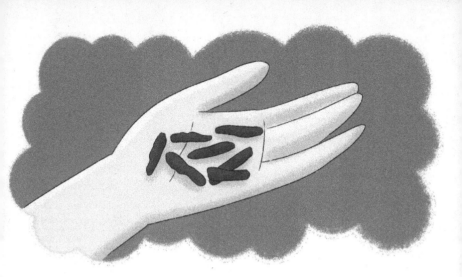

to protect the birds? It's a very important part of the food cycle."

"I'd rather have a piece of toast," Cheng chuckled.

"But seriously," Leah added with a soft voice. "We could be witnessing the death of an ecosystem here."

Beep beep.

"It's the Beagle!" Cheng said. "I wonder how it's managing to fly around here without crashing into anything."

Leah watched as it ducked low ceilings and scooted round corners. "Sonar! It's

beeping to make soundwaves, and then using soundwave location to navigate in the dark, just like bats. Well done, Beagle!"

With the Beagle trailing them, they continued to follow the markers through passages and into caverns, each one different. Some dry and empty, others dripping with water and full of incredible rock formations.

"Wow!" Cheng said, pointing his head torch up at the ceiling, where the rock looked like petrified waves.

"Do you know how many times you've said wow?" Leah laughed.

"I know, I can't help – WOW!" Cheng pointed excitedly at the yellowish boulders that lined the far end of the cavern. "See those? They're created by calcite deposits, and those channels and grooves are signs of erosion. That means two things – one, the caves are limestone, and two, this place gets a lot of water! Probably during the monsoon season."

"And where there's water, there's life," Leah said, watching as mayflies danced above their heads, their wings caught in the torches' glow.

"What are they doing down here?"

"They have a symbiotic relationship with bats," Leah explained. "That means that they need each other. Mayflies live off the fungus and algae that grows on the guano, and the mayflies are also part of the bats' diet. It's the perfect example of a balanced ecosystem. And it means one thing – you're right. Water must be nearby. It's where the mayflies lay their eggs."

A series of beeps pipped down the passageway.

"The Beagle went ahead," Cheng said. "And it sounds like it's trying to warn us."

Cheng and Leah pointed their torches ahead and followed the Beagle's beeps to the far end of the cavern, where the only way on was through a fissure – a long crack in the rock wall – a dark split that looked barely big enough for a bat.

Was it a dead end?

Chapter Four
A TIGHT SQUEEZE

Closer up, the crack was wider than it first looked – a jagged fracture that created a narrow tunnel. It was big enough to walk through, single file. Cheng peered inside.

"What can you see?" Leah asked.

Cheng stood back. "It looks as if the crack goes all the way through the rock, but there's only one way to find out, and that's to go in."

The Beagle, which had been buzzing around them, pulled in its drone wings, contracted its body to bat-size and shot into the crack.

"I guess it's leading the way," Cheng said with a shrug. "Come on. Follow me and watch your head. It looks as if the ceiling gets a bit low."

They edged into the fissure after the tiny Beagle. Walking behind Cheng, and only occasionally having to duck her head, Leah thought caving was a lot easier than it first looked. But then there was a loud beep and Cheng stopped abruptly.

"What's the matter?" said Leah, straining to see.

"The Beagle's gone ahead and is letting us know the passage is narrowing. Ow!" Cheng rubbed his head. "And it's getting lower. We'll have to go slowly and carefully."

Stooping beneath the low passage ceiling, it wasn't long before their backs began to ache.

Cheng spoke to Leah over his shoulder. "Crouch low, put your hands on your thighs, and straighten out your spine. Shuffle forward like a crouching penguin. It feels silly, but it'll take the strain off your back."

Leah followed Cheng's advice, but as the cave passage closed in tighter and tighter, from every side, they were forced to crawl on hands and knees. Leah was grateful for the kneepads. Maybe caving was as hard as she first thought, after all.

"Are you okay?" Cheng called back.

Leah sensed uncertainty in his voice, and although she was feeling a bit wobbly, she kept her voice light. "Yes, I'm fine. Are you?"

"I'm a bit worried about how narrow it's getting."

Leah took a big breath to steady her nerves. "We'll be fine, Cheng," she said brightly. Knowing he felt responsible for her safety, she needed to keep his spirits up. "You're a rock steady guide. You're stone cold brilliant."

"Very funny, Leah," Cheng said.

"You know what I like about you, Cheng? You're down to earth."

Leah heard Cheng's chuckle. "Stop making me laugh."

"Don't you just lava my jokes?"

"Yes, but it's enough now."

"Why?"

"Because we made it." Cheng whooshed a sigh of relief. "We're through to the other side."

Leah wriggled through the last tiny length of passage and stood up next to Cheng. She gasped at the cathedral-size chamber in front of them. Their torch light rippled across the wet walls, picking up mineral colours of blue and green. Lace-like seams of quartz glittered round the room, and calcite deposits created curious stacks, like tall melting candles, frozen in time.

Silenced by the awesomeness of this beautiful place, they slowly and silently high-fived.

"I'm so glad we got to see this," Leah whispered. "Thanks for bringing me here. I'd never have made it this far without your caving knowledge."

"Thank you," Cheng insisted. "If it wasn't for you keeping my spirits up, I probably wouldn't have kept going."

"So you do like my jokes," Leah said with a grin.

"They're ore-some. Get it? Ore?"

"Oh! As in a rock that contains metal or minerals! Very good, Cheng." Leah patted him on the shoulder and he did a little bow. "But we'd better put jokes aside. We need to get serious about finding the lost woman."

They searched for markers, and found three more on the floor of the cavern. It was a relief that they were still going in the right direction. All around them rose incredible rock formations. Some looked as if they had been built by wizard architects. Leah was starting to understand Cheng's fascination. She stopped to look at one that was shaped like an old church organ, with pipes rising right up to the ceiling. Then she saw the wall behind it – not smooth like the rest of the cave rock, but scratched and rough, with fresh dry rock exposed.

"Cheng, over here!" She stooped down to look at the dust on the floor. "Is there any geological explanation for this?"

Cheng furrowed his brow. "No, that's not erosion. It's too rough. It looks as if it's been dug out."

"I don't think any animal big enough to have huge claws would be down here. Wait, there's a mayfly in the dust."

Leah brushed back the crumbs. "Oh! That's not a mayfly."

She held up a small stone. It shone blue in the torch light.

"It's a sapphire!" Cheng said. "They are worth a lot of money. I mean, a lot!"

"Whoever did this was looking for sapphires," Cheng said. "They left markers so they could find their way back out."

"And they scared away the bats!" said Leah.

"They must be illegal miners." Cheng sighed.

"And eco-ignoramuses!" said Leah. And she wasn't joking.

Chapter Five

HEADING INTO DANGER

Cheng put the sapphire in his pocket. For a moment everything was quiet. Leah noticed him looking at her with worry.

"I know you're angry about the miners disturbing the bat colonies, but we need to have a calm head when we're caving."

"I know, and I'm not angry, really," Leah said with a sigh. "Not everyone understands how fragile ecosystems are. They probably didn't know. Come on, we'd better carry on with the search. Look, a marker!"

Leah bounded towards a bright green marker. Right in front of it there was another. And in front of that was a pile of rocks, blocking an exit out of the cave.

"A rockfall. From all that dust, it looks like it happened very recently," Cheng said.

"Maybe the missing woman went through this exit, and then it fell down??" said Leah.

Leah and Cheng looked at each other in dismay. They began to push the rocks aside, being careful not to cut themselves on the sharp edges, and sneezing at the dust being released. In the distance, there was a loud rumble.

"More rockfalls," he said. "That's not good."

"We have to help her," Leah insisted, pulling away a heavy rock and falling backwards.

They sat a while, overwhelmed by the task ahead. Everything was silent, apart from the dripping and the trickles from tiny streams, which tinkled like wind chimes. And then, there was another noise.

"Did you say something?" Leah asked.

"No."

"I heard something. Another rock fall

maybe." She felt her insides wobble. What if they got blocked in?

Cheng and the Beagle rushed to Leah's side and they waited quietly, listening for another noise and hoping it wasn't the sound of doom.

"There!" Leah said. "Did you hear it?"

"Helloooooooo – ooo – ooo."

"Three voices – perhaps it's Hunar's tourist group."

"No, not three voices. One voice, echoing," Leah said.

"Heeeeeeelp – elp – elp."

"You're right. Someone is in trouble," Cheng agreed. "It must be the missing woman! I wonder if she's the one stealing sapphires?"

"Either way, she must be very scared. Let's tell her we're here." Leah lifted the whistle on the string around her neck and gave three short peeps.

"Yes – es – es! Helloooo – ooo – ooo! I'm here – ere – ere."

"She heard us," Cheng said excitedly. "But we can't get past the rock fall. We'll have to go back and see if we can find another route. Blow the whistle again. If she keeps responding we'll be able to locate her better."

Leah peeped her whistle, and Cheng led the way back across the cavern. As Leah looked around the cave one more time, she spotted another marker. Then another. They pointed to a recess at the back of the cavern – an area they hadn't investigated.

"Cheng, look!" Leah cried. "She isn't behind the rockfall. She must have been stopped by the falling rock and decided to go this way!"

Cheng pointed his beam at the back wall. "Another fissure," he said excitedly.

Cheng entered, beckoning eagerly – it wasn't as tricky as the first fissure they'd encountered.

"Hellooooooo – ooo – ooo."

"We're coming!" Leah shouted.

The further they edged through the crack, the clearer the woman's voice became.

"Can you hear us?" Leah called.

"Yes! Loud and clear!" said the woman.

"We must be close," Cheng said.

"Don't panic!" Leah shouted. "We'll find you."

The Beagle buzzed ahead and then buzzed back again, bouncing up and down, beeping repeatedly.

"I think there's something dangerous ahead," Cheng said. "We'd better walk slowly."

"I'm down here!" came the voice.

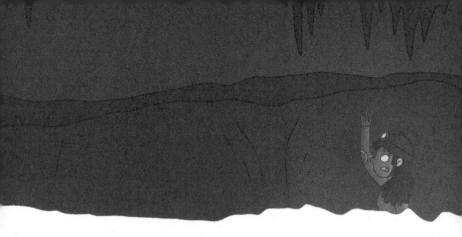

"Down?" Leah said. "That doesn't sound good."

"It isn't." Cheng held his arm out to stop Leah getting too close.

She shuffled forward and then gasped. They were on a high ledge, close to the ceiling of a vast cavern – bigger than any they had seen – and below them was a sheer drop to the cave floor. They could just about make out the woman. Her headlamp was dim – the battery was low.

"We're here," Leah called. "We'll throw down a rope!"

"I can't climb," the woman wailed. "I've hurt my ankle. Please don't leave me!"

"Of course we won't leave you. We'll come down!" Leah said. She turned to Cheng. "How are we going to get down to her? It's a big drop."

Cheng responded with a grin. "Rappelling," he said. "When I saw the equipment we'd been given, I had a feeling that we'd be doing this."

"What is rappelling?" Leah said, worriedly.

"It's fun, that's what it is," said Cheng. He thought for a moment. "As long as we're really, really careful."

"What you just said does not fill me with

confidence," Leah said, peering over the edge once more.

"You'll be fine, I promise." Cheng took the ropes from their backpacks and placed them on the floor. "I've done this with my parents loads of times." He held up the end of a rope that had a pointed barb attached to it. "See this? I'm going to wedge it in a really secure place so it can take our weight."

Cheng spotted a small gap in the wall behind and angled the barb into it, before tugging the rope and wedging it securely. He pulled and pulled until he was certain that the rope was not going to spring free.

"That's the anchor sorted. Now, while I get the friction hitches ready, get into your harness. The straps circle your thighs."

"What are friction hitches?" asked Leah, trying to cover her fear with curiosity.

"They are the knots that will hold you in case you slip," he explained.

Leah looked at him worriedly but he nodded that it was all going to be okay.

When she had tightened the harness, Cheng hooked ropes between the harness, the hitch, and the climbing rope with a secure metal karabiner clip – an oval clasp that could only be opened by applying pressure from the outside. He handed her a length of rope.

"Hold this out at an angle behind and below you. When you pull on it, you'll slow down. It works like a brake. Now you'll be able to walk down the wall at your own speed. When you've reached the bottom, I'll use the rope to come down. I'll be watching you every step of the way."

Leah nodded. She was nervous, but Cheng sounded as if he knew exactly what he was doing.

"Remember, lean back and bend your legs, and walk backwards. Feed the rope through your hand, and when you want to go more slowly, just remember to pull the brake rope. Ready?"

Leah leaned back over the edge, amazed at how secure she felt. Slowly, she backed over the cliff and began to walk down, hand quite relaxed on the brake cord as she found herself enjoying it.

"This is amazing!" she called.

"Told you," Cheng cheered. "When you've unhooked yourself, tug the rope to let me know it's free."

Leah, placing one foot behind the other, walked the entire wall without stopping. At the bottom she unclipped her harness and tugged the rope. "All yours, Cheng!" she called, finding it hard to hide the delight in her voice. That was amazing! She ran to where the woman was waiting.

Leah had assumed the woman was old, but she realised now that the lines she thought were deep wrinkles were streaks of grime. Her face and hands were covered in slime from the wet rock, and her tatty clothes – a loose top and wide-legged trousers – had almost lost their colour beneath the filth. It looked as if she had nothing with her for protection, although she did have a bag. Leah wondered if there might be something useful inside, but the woman groaned and she turned back.

"I'm Leah. Can you tell me your name?"

"Zara." The woman tried to get up again, but her ankle

crumpled and she fell back down. "I can't get up."

"Did you fall, Zara?" Leah said. She noticed the ankle was swollen.

"I tripped and it got caught on a rock and twisted. I think it is sprained. It hurts." Zara winced.

"Let me see if I've got anything that might help," Leah said. "Sit down and put your leg out straight." She opened her backpack, pulled out a first aid kit, and thought back to the first aid lessons she'd had at school. "Numbing spray and bandages! Excellent." She bound the woman's ankle over and over so it wouldn't move. "It's a really good job we found you," she said as she worked. "You were never going to get very far on this."

The woman looked at her strangely. "Yes, thank you. But who are you?"

Leah smiled. "We're, um, people who solve problems. And this is a big one."

There was a crunch as Cheng landed at the bottom of the rock face. "How is she?" he said.

"Cheng, this is Zara."

Zara smiled meekly. "And who is he?"

"That's Cheng." Leah looked up at her Explorer friend. "It looks like she has a sprained ankle, but I've bandaged it tightly and I think we're ready to go."

"Good, we should get out of here as soon as possible. If there's been one rock fall there could be another."

Cheng and Leah helped Zara to her feet and propped her up.

"Wait!" Zara hobbled back to fetch her backpack. As she tried to swing it onto her shoulder, a cascade of sapphires spilled from its opening.

Chapter Six
THE PRICE OF PRECIOUS STONES

Leah and Cheng were speechless as Zara dropped to her knees, scrabbling to collect them all.

"Leave them," Cheng said sternly.

"No. They're mine. I worked hard for them!"

"Did you know that your illegal mining is ruining these caves!" Leah blurted.

"I am deep underground where no one can see," Zara protested. "I'm not hurting anyone."

"But you are!" Leah said. "'You're making the caves unstable and hurting the animals that need the caves for shelter and food! You're killing a whole ecosystem!"

The woman looked up and blinked as if she didn't understand.

"Tell her about the bats," Cheng said.

Leah pointed to the ceiling. "Up there, there should be colonies of bats. But they're either being scared away or they're dying because of fungus and bacteria brought in from outside. If they disappear, so will the insects and the algae and the bacteria that live down here. The cave system is unique. When you mine illegally, you're treading on this precious little planet!"

Leah realized she been waving her arms about, and quickly crossed them in front of her. The woman stood up.

"I am really sorry to hear that," she said.

Leah softened. "Perhaps now you understand how fragile this place is, you'll leave it alone in future?"

"I cannot do that." The woman looked down, embarrassed. "I need the money. Everything I make from selling these sapphires, I send to my grandparents. They are poor and have no way of working to support themselves. Please don't report me."

Leah and Cheng looked at each other. Their shoulders dropped in despair. This was a lot more complicated than they'd realized.

"Right now, the important thing is to get you to safety," said Leah. "Come on, we'll help you over to the ropes and then we can—"

There was a sudden crash – a boom, like thunder echoing in a mountain valley. Dust rained down on their heads. Cheng wiped his eyes and looked up.

"Oh no! Quickly, back away, back away. A rockfall!"

Cheng and Leah ducked beneath Zara's shoulders to support her weight and they hurried away from the rock face. Their soles slipped on the slimy, uneven floor, and as Leah's boot skidded into one of the many divots, she realised how easy it would be to twist an ankle, or worse. Small rocks, dislodged by the unfolding catastrophe above, skittered like marbles across the floor in front of them.

"Hurry!" Cheng shouted.

With one last push, they got to the middle of the cavern, where they collapsed in a heap. More rocks dropped and bounced down the cliff, some as big as cars. When the tumbling had stopped, they looked up at the ledge they'd rappelled down from.

It was covered in rubble and the entrance to the cave behind it was completely blocked.

"You'll know some clever trick to get us out of here, right?" Leah tried a big grin, but it faded when she saw the horror on Cheng's face. "This is really bad, isn't it?"

"Yep."

There was a loud buzz as the Beagle, which had been motionless during the conversation with Zara, suddenly took off.

"What is that?" Zara shrieked.

"It's the Beagle," Leah said.

"It doesn't look like a dog," Zara said. "And I've never heard of a flying dog!"

"It's a drone. Beagle is just its name," said Leah, watching it fly towards to the back of the cave and then out of sight. "I wonder where it's going?"

It returned instantly and circled the group.

"I think it wants to show us something," Cheng said. "Go on Beagle, what have you got?"

The Beagle turned and projected an image onto the wall. It was a cave – a different one to the one they were in.

"You've been exploring, Beagle!" Cheng said. "Zoom in. Show us more detail."

The image on the wall grew larger and larger until they could see the shape of the cavern. It had a low ceiling, and, as the image panned round, they could see how craggy it was – full of trip hazards. And the only entrance appeared to be a narrow fissure.

"No thanks, Beagle!" Cheng said. "I've had enough of tiny spaces today. Are there any more?"

The Beagle flashed up another picture. This time it was a huge chamber, and the Beagle's lights flickered off the ceiling and glistened on the wet floor.

"That one looks a big soggy," Leah said.

"I know what that is!" Zara said, brightly. "That's not a wet floor, it's a lake! A mining friend told me about underwater lakes in this cave network. I never came across one so I didn't believe him."

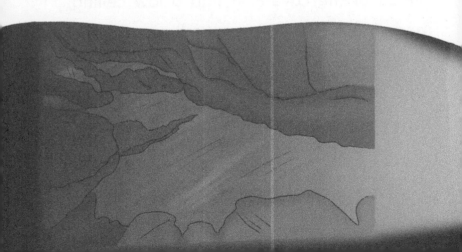

"Closer, Beagle!" Cheng said, excitedly.

The Beagle made the picture bigger, and the full size of the lake became clear. It was huge, and filled the floor of the cave. Around it, just above the waterlines, there were eroded grooves and ledges, like open passageways that stretched all the way round the room. It looked as if there were plenty of entrances and exits leading in and out.

"Wow, it's beautiful," Leah said. "Are there any fish in there, do you think?"

"Don't ask me, I'm the rocks, guy," Cheng said.

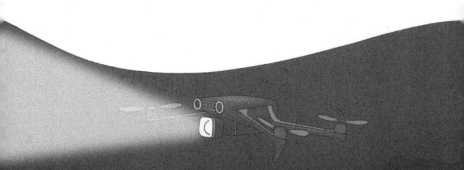

Cheng looked up once again at the rock fall on the ledge. "That fall could trigger more. I think the lake cave is our safest bet. Show us the way!"

The Beagle pipped with excitement. Helping Zara and taking it slowly, they shuffled after the Beagle, which led them to the far end of the cavern. There, nestled behind a crop of stalagmites, was another hidden passageway.

It led them to another small cavern where they took another passage.

"Shhh!" Leah said, and they stopped mid-way. "I can hear water."

There had been lots of trickles along the way, and Cheng had explained that the stalagmites they'd seen were the result of water on the ceiling dripping calcite. But this sound was different. There were plops and bubbles, and occasionally a small splash. Was it rain?

Thinking there might be an exit to above-ground, they hurried as quickly as Zara's ankle would allow. The passage led to yet another cave. It was the one the Beagle had shown them, and they found themselves on one of the ledges, overlooking a large lake. Their torchlight illuminated the water. It was bright blue and crystal clear.

"This would be a good place to rest a moment, if you don't mind," Zara said.

"Of course," said Cheng.

Zara sat on a rock ledge while Leah and Cheng stretched out their backs and looked around at the incredible lake in front of them.

"Amazing colours," Leah sighed.

"It's probably mineral deposits," Cheng said, angling his torch down into the water.

Then Leah saw something dart beneath the surface – bright, like a shooting star. At first she thought it was a trick on the water, created by her helmet torch, but then she saw more. And more.

"Fish!" Leah exclaimed. "Underground fish! I can't believe it!"

"I thought you'd have known that cave

lakes had fish," Cheng teased.

"I did!" Leah laughed. "But I never thought I'd actually see them."

Cheng and Leah lay flat on their stomachs and peered into the lake, spotting small white and silver fish. The water was so clear they could see every scale and fin. The Cheng scrambled back from the edge in horror.

"They've got no eyes!" he gasped.

"Don't worry, it's totally normal for

creatures to adapt to their environment," Leah said, in a matter of fact voice. "And as there's no light down there, they don't need eyes... Isn't it amazing? Nature is so clever."

Zara appeared alongside. "That's so interesting! I can't wait to tell my grandparents. They live on the coast and when I visit them, I always spend time in the sea. I love marine life."

"You'd love our friend Connor," Cheng said. "He knows a lot about oceans."

They watched the fish for a bit longer, pointing out the occasional pink-coloured one, and remarking on the strangeness of their closed-up eyes. Then Cheng's torchlight began to flicker – a sign

that the battery was starting to run out.

"The last thing we want is to be sightless here," he said. "The fish are used to it, but we're not. We'd better get going."

The hollows they'd thought were passages on the Beagle's picture turned out to be shallow caves. The only way out of the lake cave was through a tunnel at the end.

"If we go that way, it'll just lead us deeper into the system," Zara said shakily.

"I've got a horrible feeling that we're just getting further and further away from the open air, and more and more lost."

The Beagle beeped loudly in agreement.

"The way back is blocked by the rock fall," Cheng said. "We don't have much choice."

Chapter Seven
SEEING IS BELIEVING

Silence fell over the cave as they considered their situation.

"Come on," Leah said, forcing herself to be optimistic. "There's no point thinking the worst. And who knows what we'll find along the way!"

"You are right," said Zara. "Losing hope is sometimes the worst thing to do. Let's go. Cheng, are you okay?"

Cheng was looking around him, like an amazed astronomer looking at the cosmos. "Just taking in some of the sights, so I don't forget them," he said.

They edged along the groove, following the Beagle through the narrow exit passage that wound deeper and deeper into the earth. It eventually reached another cavern with various pools that had formed either side of rock deposits.

"There are fish here, too," said Leah, peering in.

The light from her head torch pierced the clear water and tickled a shoal of small white fish, similar to the ones they'd seen before. They darted away into the shadows.

"Wait!" Leah said. She crouched by the edge of the pool and watched as the fish moved away from her beam. "Look. They're swimming away. They're avoiding the light. That means, they must either sense it, or they can see it."

"But we're still underground," Cheng said. "I don't see how any light could get in."

"I know. It's a mystery. But it must mean that there's something special about this cave," Leah insisted. "I just have a feeling that if we found out why this is happening, it could help us. Think, think!"

"*I think,*" Cheng said with a wide grin, "that it might be time to call our friends."

"Of course, the rest of the Secret Explorers!" Leah said.

"'Secret Explorers'?" Zara put her head to one side. "What is this 'Secret Explorers'?"

"It's the name of the organization of helpers I was telling you about. There are a few of us – all the others are back at headquarters."

"Beagle!" Cheng called. "Alert the Exploration Station!"

The Beagle, which had been hovering over the water taking photos of the lake for Cheng's research, landed at their feet. There was clunking and whirring as its metal plates expanded to create a small table-like structure. Then a screen flipped up. On it were the six friendly faces of the Secret Explorers.

"Hi, Leah! Hi, Cheng!" they all called.

"Hi, gang," said Leah. "We are so pleased to see you!"

"Where are you?" Roshni said. "You look like you're in space."

"We're in a dark place, that's for sure. And we can't seem to find a way out of it," said Cheng. "But Leah has some questions."

"Go on, Leah – we're ready," said Kiki. "What's the question?"

"Well, we found a cave lake full of fish with no eyes, which is understandable. They've adapted to the darkness over time. But now we're in a cave that's quite similar, but the fish are reacting to our lights. I can't help feeling it's important."

"Hi, Leah, it's Connor here." Connor's face appeared at the centre of the screen.

"Is that the one you were telling me about?" Zara said. "I'm excited to hear what he says."

"Go on, Connor," Cheng said.

"I've read about this phenomenon. Eyeless fish do react to light, but only if they've encountered it before. Which must mean that in the cave you're in, people have already passed through with torches. I hope that helps."

"Yes!" Leah clapped her hands. "You've been a huge help as always, Secret Explorers! We'd better go."

The Secret Explorers waved. *"Bye!"* they chorused, and continued to beam happily until the screen went blank.

The Beagle folded down the screen, contracted back to its bat-drone shape, and beeped three times.

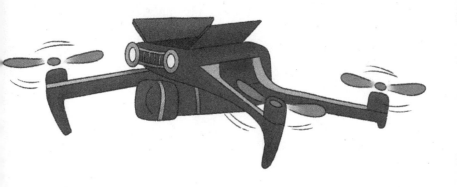

"I'm excited, too, Beagle," replied Leah.

"Why?" Cheng asked. "They didn't give us any information that could show us how to get out of here."

"Yes they did. Don't you see?" Leah said, jumping up and down on her toes with excitement.

"No, we are like the first fish," Zara said, and she and Cheng laughed and shook their heads.

"Let me explain," said Leah. "If these fish sense light, it means enough people with torches have come this way before. And I don't see any skeletons round here, so it means they found a way out."

"They probably had a map," Cheng said.

"And we have fish!" said Leah. "In every cave we enter, we do the light test. If the fish swim away then we know that's the route the people used."

"Brilliant, Leah!" said Cheng.

"So young and so clever," Zara said, shaking her head with disbelief.

They made their way through the caverns, sweeping their torches over the water of the subterranean lakes, looking for the fishes' reaction. Whenever the fish darted away, they high-fived their discovery and kept on going. They were filled with hope. They were getting somewhere!

And then, they reached a cavern where there were no lakes. In fact, there was barely a trickle of water.

"This is a problem," Cheng said. "Without the fish to show us the way, we're in the dark again, not knowing which way to turn."

"You could send your Beagle friend to see," suggested Zara.

"No, wait!" Leah held up her hand and

slowly brushed the air above her head with her fingers.

"Does she want another high-five?" Zara quizzed.

"I feel a breeze! Come on, this way!"

Chapter Eight
THE GREAT BAT ESCAPE

They moved through the next passage to another dry, lake-less cave. Cheng groaned in disappointment. "Perhaps you were dreaming it out of desperation, like how people who are lost in the desert sometimes imagine they see an oasis."

"Yes, she could be seeing things," Zara nodded, solemnly.

"I am seeing something, actually," Leah said. "Look up."

Above their heads, a colony of dark furry pods began to shift and squeak. Some let go with their toes and began to flap above their heads, their leathery wings snapping open like umbrellas.

"It must be dusk," Leah said. "They'll be leaving the caves to feed on insects – we can follow them out, but we'll have to be quick."

With Zara's ankle now very swollen, Leah and Cheng took most of her weight on their shoulders. They were all tired, but the thought of finding a way out gave them an extra boost. And the Beagle swooped and pipped in their ears, telling them to hurry.

The bats poured through a channel that led out of the cave, and Leah, Cheng, and Zara had to keep their heads low to avoid the winged bustle as they followed. The passage began to rise on an incline and then, quite suddenly, they emerged into the dusky evening, ears ringing with the flap and squeak of frantic bats, and cool night air rippling through their hair. They were out!

"You!"

They turned to see Hunar, running towards them.

"Hi, Hunar," Cheng said. "We're pleased to see you. We found the missing person, but she's injured."

Hunar clearly had many questions, but he looked at Zara's bandaged foot and quickly nodded. "Stay. I'll go and call for help."

Hunar ran towards the caving centre, shouting commands through his radio. The kids sat on the ground, breathing in the night air until it filled their lungs.

"I'm sorry," said Zara, softly. "I feel terrible about everything I put you through. And for the mining. Without the creatures of the caves, we'd never have got out alive. Following the bats, and before that, seeing the sightless fish."

"You didn't know," Cheng said, kindly.

"Even I've learned new things about ecosystems today," Leah said.

"I will find another way to make some money," said Zara. "And I will tell all the other miners, too. Humans are one of the most resourceful animals – we can work out another way to make a living."

Leah gave Zara a big hug. "I'm so pleased, Zara. Perhaps now the bats will return and the caves will thrive, and I just know that you'll find a way one day."

"Maybe there's a way right now," Cheng said, standing. He paced. "Hunar said the caving centre needed staff, didn't he? And who better to show tourists than you, Zara? You're an experienced caver, and you'll be able to tell them all about the bats and fish. Here's Hunar, now."

Hunar returned with news that an ambulance was on the way. He helped Zara to her feet and as they hobbled towards the road, Leah and Cheng could hear them discussing their love of the caves. Before they vanished from sight, Zara turned and waved at them.

"Hunar has just offered me a job as a tour guide!" she shouted.

"That's great news, Zara!" Cheng whooped.

"Bye, Zara! Good luck!" Leah called. She sighed happily. "I think our work here is done," she said, raising her hand in a high-five.

Cheng ducked his hand out of the way. "Feel the breeze!" he teased. "Hey, where's the Beagle?"

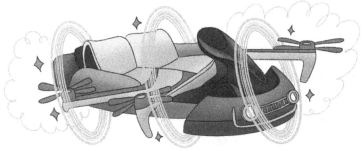

They found it behind a rock, mid-transformation. Metal plates and panels puffed out from the drone, expanding rapidly until it was go-kart shaped once again. Then wheels popped out from underneath its floor.

Beep beep!

They leapt into the familiar battered seats, and the Beagle was off, accelerating into a bright white light, leaving the caves and its inhabitants behind.

A few moments later, the light vanished and Leah and Cheng blinked as they settled into their surroundings. Six faces appeared around them.

"Well done!" cheered Ollie.

"Mission accomplished," said Tamiko. "Did you see any dinosaurs?"

"No, but we saw some awesome eyeless fish," Cheng said.

"We've got so much to tell you," Leah said.

"And show you." Cheng pulled the sapphire from his pocket and held it up to the light. It shimmered royal blue. "This is going in the display," he said, leaping out of the Beagle and placing it gently on a glass shelf. "Another Secret Explorer treasure."

"But the real treasure was the ecosystem," Leah said. "The incredible species that make a life in the darkness."

"Time for us all to go home," Leah said. "See you next time, friends."

She gave a wave and stepped through the glowing door, right back into her garden shed.

Outside, the sky was dusky blue, just as it had been when she left. She made her way up the garden and, just as she passed the bat boxes, little winged critters filled the sky around her. Bats! Leah stood absolutely still and watched as they swooped and darted, catching their food. They were almost as small as mice. Teeny tiny bats.

Pipistrelle bats, Leah realised. *I have pipistrelles living in my garden!*

"You might be small but you play a huge part in our ecosystem," she marvelled. "And it's been very nice to 'squeak' to you."

Leah chuckled at her own joke and wondered what other incredible creatures she was yet to encounter as a member of the Secret Explorers.

LEAH'S
MISSION NOTES

THE HORSESHOE BAT

* **LATIN NAME:** Rhinolophidae

* **ANIMAL TYPE:** Mammal

* **LOCATION:** Horseshoe bats live
  in tropical and temperate regions,
  and have been found in Europe,
  Asia, Africa, and Oceania.

* **LENGTH:** They are an average
  of 3–11 cm (1.2–4.3 in) long.

Shap claws give the horsesh
bat a strong grip when
hanging upside down.

A BOUNTY OF BATS
Bats are the second largest group of mammals
after rodents. There are more than 1,300
different types of bats worldwide.

Bats are the only mammals
that are capable of flying.

The horseshoe bat is named after the horseshoe-
shaped growth on its nose, which amplifies the
sound it makes during echolocation.

Bats fly at night and use echolocation to find
their prey. They make ultrasonic, high-pitched
chirps that bounce off the prey and help the
bats to locate it in the darkness.

EXPLORING CAVES

Caving, or spelunking, is the exploration of caves, usually as part of a group, and led by a guide. Caving can be dangerous, so cavers must be trained and follow special safety guidelines.

CAVING EQUIPMENT

It varies depending on the type of cave, but cavers need to bring lots of specific items with them for safety.

HELMET   TORCH   ROPE   LADDER

GLOVES   HARNESS   BOOTS   RADIO

CAVE SCIENCE

Speleology is the scientific study and exploration of caves. Cave archaeologists study the evidence of early human life in caves, and cave biologists study the unique flora and fauna that live in these underground spaces.

HANG SON ĐOÒNG, VIETNAM

This is the largest cave in the world. It's so big it has a forest, a river, and even clouds inside!

MAMMOTH CAVE NATIONAL PARK, USA

At over 400 miles (644 km) long, this is the longest cave system in the world. It would take five days of non-stop walking to travel through!

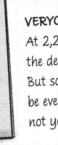

VERYOVKINA CAVE, GEORGIA

At 2,212 m (7,257 ft), this is the deepest-known cave on Earth. But scientists believe there may be even deeper caves that have not yet been discovered.

LIVING IN THE DARK

All life depends on sunlight to survive, and this is true even for the life found in the deepest, darkest caves (known as the dark zone). No green plants can grow in the dark zone, so how do the organisms that live there, survive?

THE CAVE FOOD PYRAMID

The organisms in a cave exist in a hierarchy called an ecological pyramid. At the bottom of the pyramid, organic material provides food for bacteria, which is then eaten by small insects. These small insects are eaten by bigger insects, and then the largest predators at the top of the pyramid eat these!

A large food source for cave organisms is guano (bat poo). The bacteria and fungi in caves decompose the poo into food and nutrients.

Another way food can enter caves is through floods. Excess rainwater runs into caves, bringing plants with it, providing food for insects and other animals.

Salamanders and cave centipedes

Cave spiders and fish

Bigger insects, such as cave beetles

Millipedes and crustaceans

Fungus and microscopic bacteria

Guano (bat poo), other animal droppings, and washed-in plants

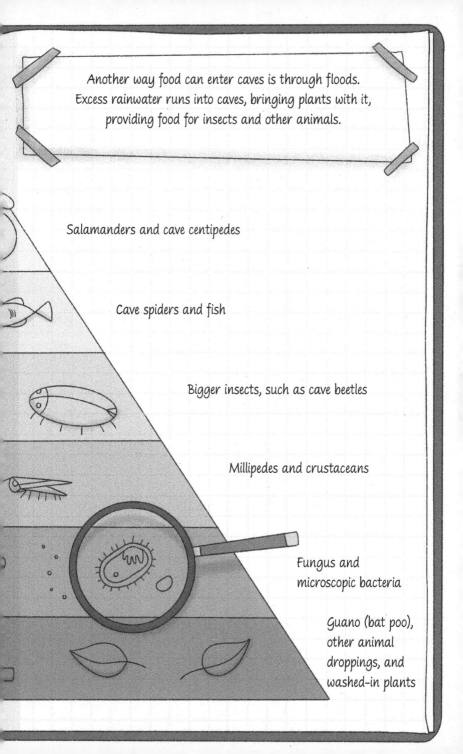

QUIZ

1   What precious gemstones were the illegal miners searching for?

2   True or false: Bats are the only mammals that can fly.

3   Bat poo is known by what other name?

4   What is the name for the special technique that bats use to find their way in the darkness.

5   True or false: There are more than 10,000 species of bat.

6   What do experienced cavers use to make sure they can retrace their path?

7   True or false: Caving can be dangerous, and should only be done with proper training or with an experienced guide.

Check your answers on page 127

GLOSSARY

BOULDER
A very large rock.

CALCITE
A common mineral substance that makes up rock formations in caves.

CHAMBER
A large open area inside a cave.

COLONY
The term used for a group of bats living together.

DRONE
Flying machine with no pilot.

ECOSYSTEM
A community of living things and their environment.

EROSION
Gradual wearing away of rocks due to water and weather. Erosion happens over a long period of time.

FERTILIZER

A substance added to soil that helps plants grow better.

FISSURE

A split or crack in the face of rocks.

GUANO

The poo of bats and some sea birds.

GUIDE

A person who leads groups of people or provides information.

KARABINER

A tool used by rock climbers.

MARKER

An object used to mark out a path.

MONSOON

A seasonal change that brings strong winds and heavy rain.

ORE

A rock that contains metal or minerals

PETRIFIED
An object that has been turned to stone.

RAPPEL
Using rope to climb down a vertical or near-vertical drop.

ROCKFALL
Rocks that have fallen away from a wall or cliff.

SAPPHIRE
A precious and valuable gemstone, usually blue.

STALACTITE
Mineral deposits that grow down from the ceiling of a cave.

STALAGMITE
Mineral deposits that grow up from the floor of a cave.

SYMBIOTIC
A type of relationship where different living things can benefit and help each other.